FEB 2 1 2011

BATMAN FELINE FELONIES

BY **JOHN SAZAKLIS**

ILLUSTRATED BY **STEVEN E. GORDON**

BATMAN created by Bob Kane
WONDER WOMAN created by William Moulton Marston

HARPER FESTIVAL
An Imprint of HarperCollinsPublishers

HarperFestival is an imprint of HarperCollins Publishers.

Batman: Feline Felonies
For information address HarperCollins Children's Books, a division of HarperCollins Publishers,
10 East 53rd Street, New York, NY 10022.
www.harpercollinschildrens.com

Library of Congress catalog card number: 2009943950
ISBN 978-0-06-188528-0
Book design by John Sazaklis
10 11 12 13 CWM 10 9 8 7 6 5 4 3 2
❖
First Edition

THE HEROES AND VILLAINS IN THIS BOOK!

BATMAN

After being orphaned as a child, young Bruce Wayne vowed to fight crime and injustice throughout Gotham City, and so he became Batman! With his high-tech crime-fighting gadgets and his armored Batmobile, Batman fears no foe and is widely known as the world's greatest detective.

WONDER WOMAN

Born on Paradise Island, home of the Amazons, Wonder Woman was given the gifts of great wisdom, strength, beauty, and speed by the ancient Greek gods. Using her Invisible Jet, magic lasso, and unbreakable silver bracelets, she fights for peace and justice.

CATWOMAN

Gotham's resident cat burglar, Catwoman steals from the rich and keeps the loot for herself. She is an expert at hand-to-hand combat, and she uses her claws and whip to pull off her cat-themed capers.

THE CHEETAH

While searching for ancient treasures to bring herself fame and fortune, archaeologist Dr. Barbara Ann Minerva unleashed a curse that gave her incredible strength and super-speed—and transformed her into the evil Cheetah!

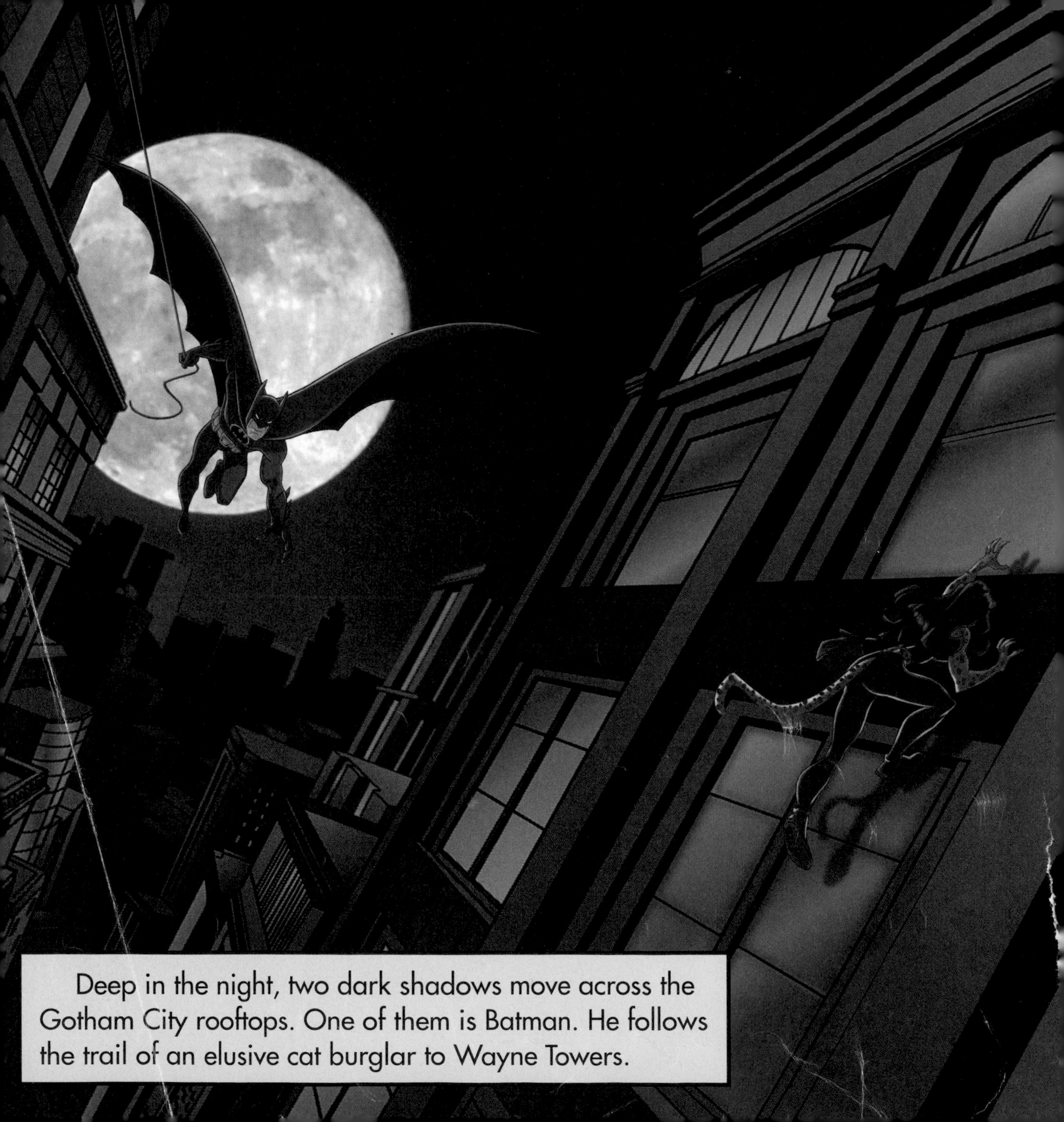

Deep in the night, two dark shadows move across the Gotham City rooftops. One of them is Batman. He follows the trail of an elusive cat burglar to Wayne Towers.

Batman lands on the balcony of the penthouse. In it is the Golden Cat, a statue so rare and valuable few have ever even seen it. Only one thief in Gotham would dare try to pull off such a cat-themed robbery.

"It ends here, Catwoman!" growls the Caped Crusader.

The thief steps into the moonlight. But it's not Catwoman . . . it's the Cheetah!
Batman is stunned.

"They say you're the world's greatest detective, but I'm not impressed,"
hisses the feline felon. "Out of my way. I've got a city to rob!"

The Cheetah tries to slash Batman with her sharp claws, but he uses his cape to protect himself.

With catlike speed, the Cheetah leaps off the balcony into the darkness. Batman quickly throws a Bat-Tracker onto the escaping villainess.

The Caped Crusader contacts Wonder Woman from his Batmobile.
"Your archenemy almost made me her new scratching post," Batman says.
"The Cheetah is in Gotham?" Wonder Woman asks. "I'm on my way!"

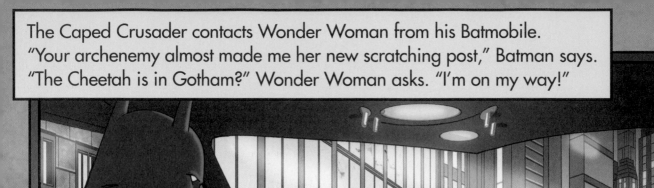

Minutes later, Wonder Woman lands her Invisible Jet on the
roof of the Gotham City Museum, where Batman is waiting for her.

"My Bat-Tracker led me here," says Batman.
"The Cat's Eye Opal is on display and worth millions."
"Let's pounce!" Wonder Woman replies.

The Cheetah breaks into the dark museum only o discover that Gotham City's original cat burglar, Catwoman, is already on the scene . . . and she has her paws on the famous gem!

"And who might you be?" Catwoman asks.

"I'm the Cheetah," says the villainess. "And you're stealing my Cat's Eye!"

Catwoman raises her claws and hisses. "Come any closer, and this won't be the only cat's eye you lose!"

"Mee-ouch!" the Cheetah snaps back.

The night watchmen hear the catfight and sound the alarm.

"Time to crash this party!" Batman says.

"Look what the Cheetah dragged in!" Catwoman snarls.
The Caped Crusader and the Amazon Princess face off against their feline foes.
The cat burglars have to work together to get out of this tight spot.

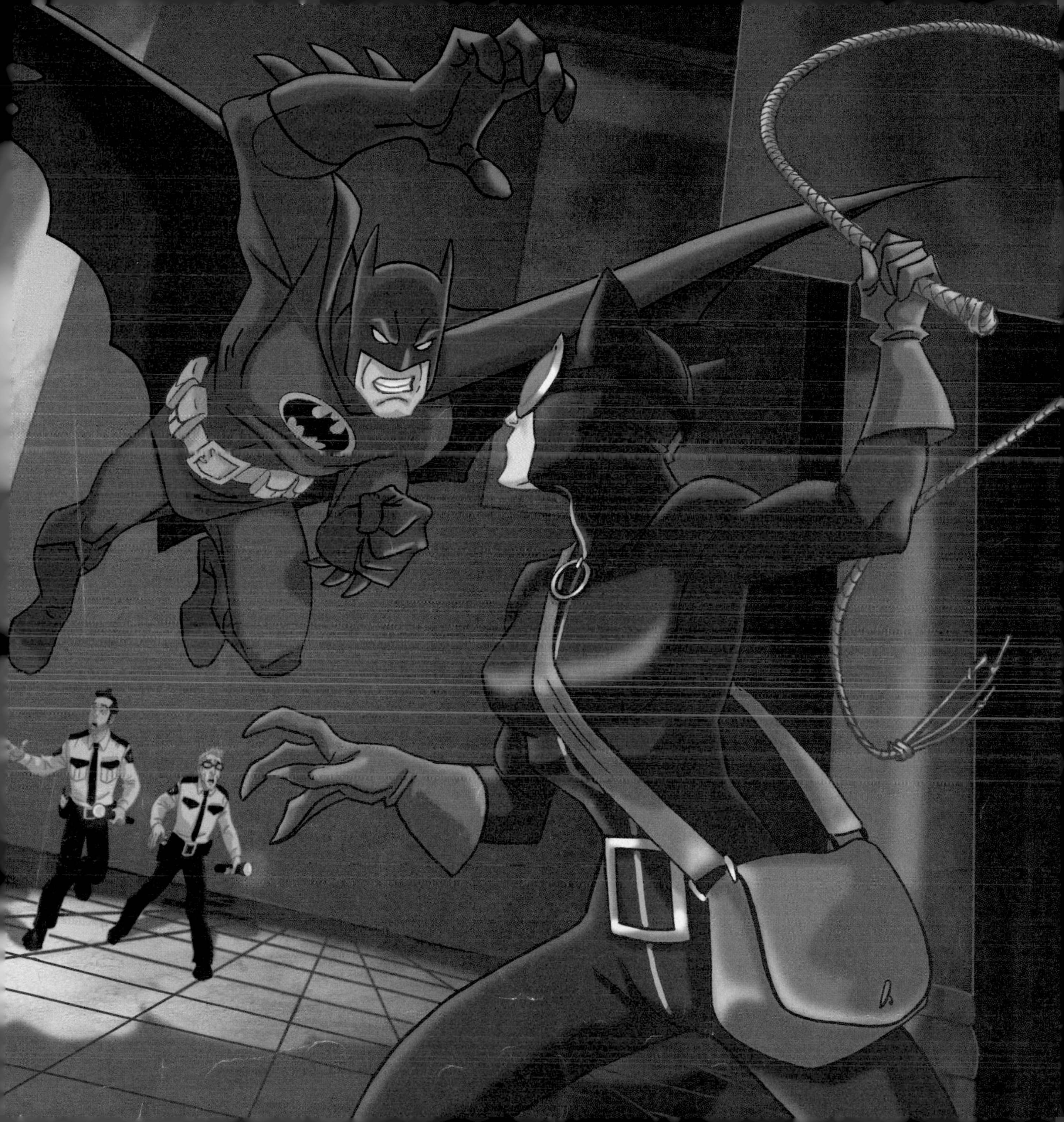

The Cheetah and Catwoman grab the guards and take them hostage.
"Not another step," the Cheetah yells.
"Or else!" Catwoman finishes.
The heroes must allow the criminals to go, in order to save the hostages.

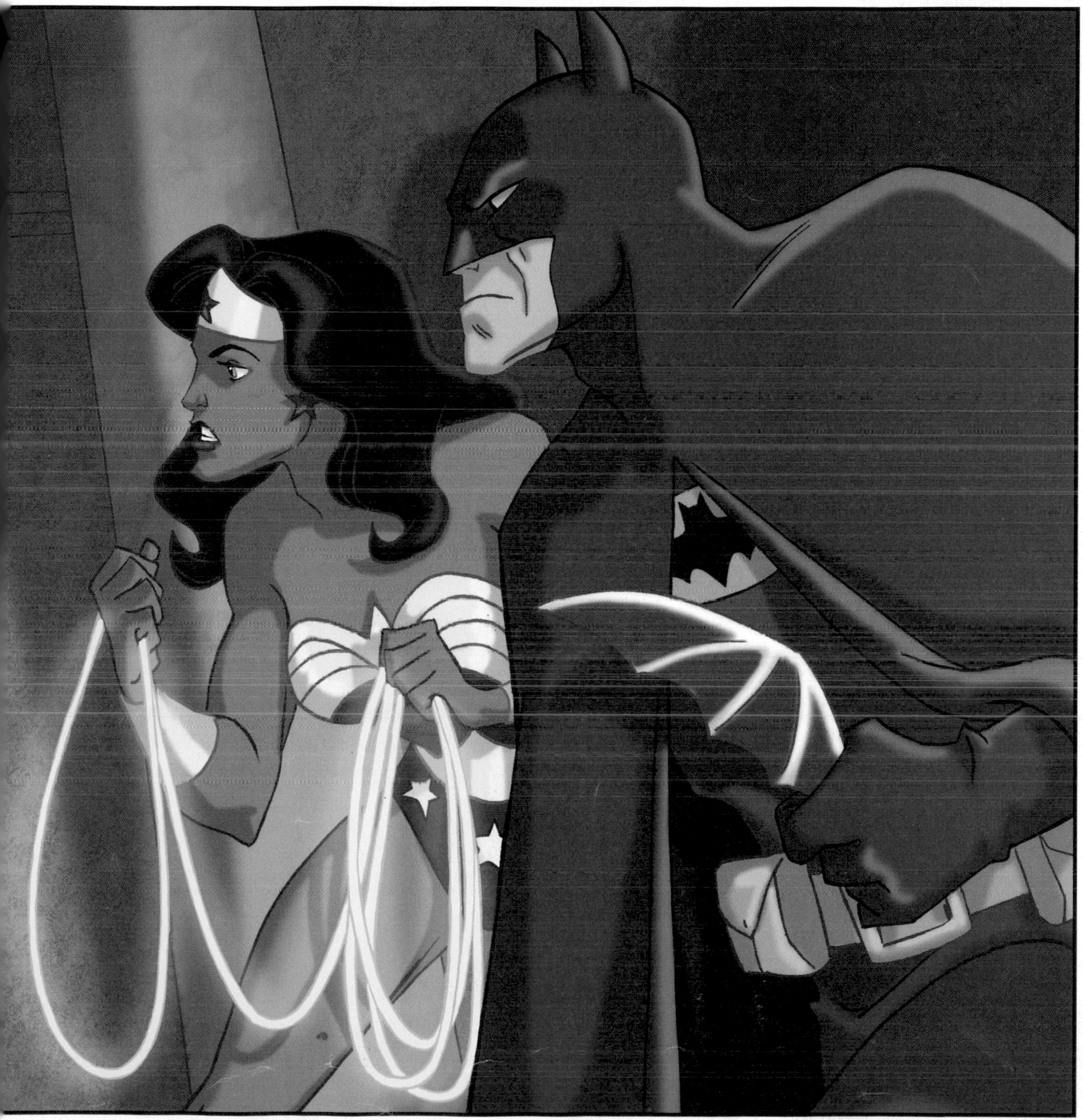

Back on the roof, Batman is angry at this turn of events.

"We can still find them with your Bat-Tracker," Wonder Woman says.

"That's true," says Batman. "I have a plan." He looks at the Invisible Jet and smiles. "They won't know what hit them!"

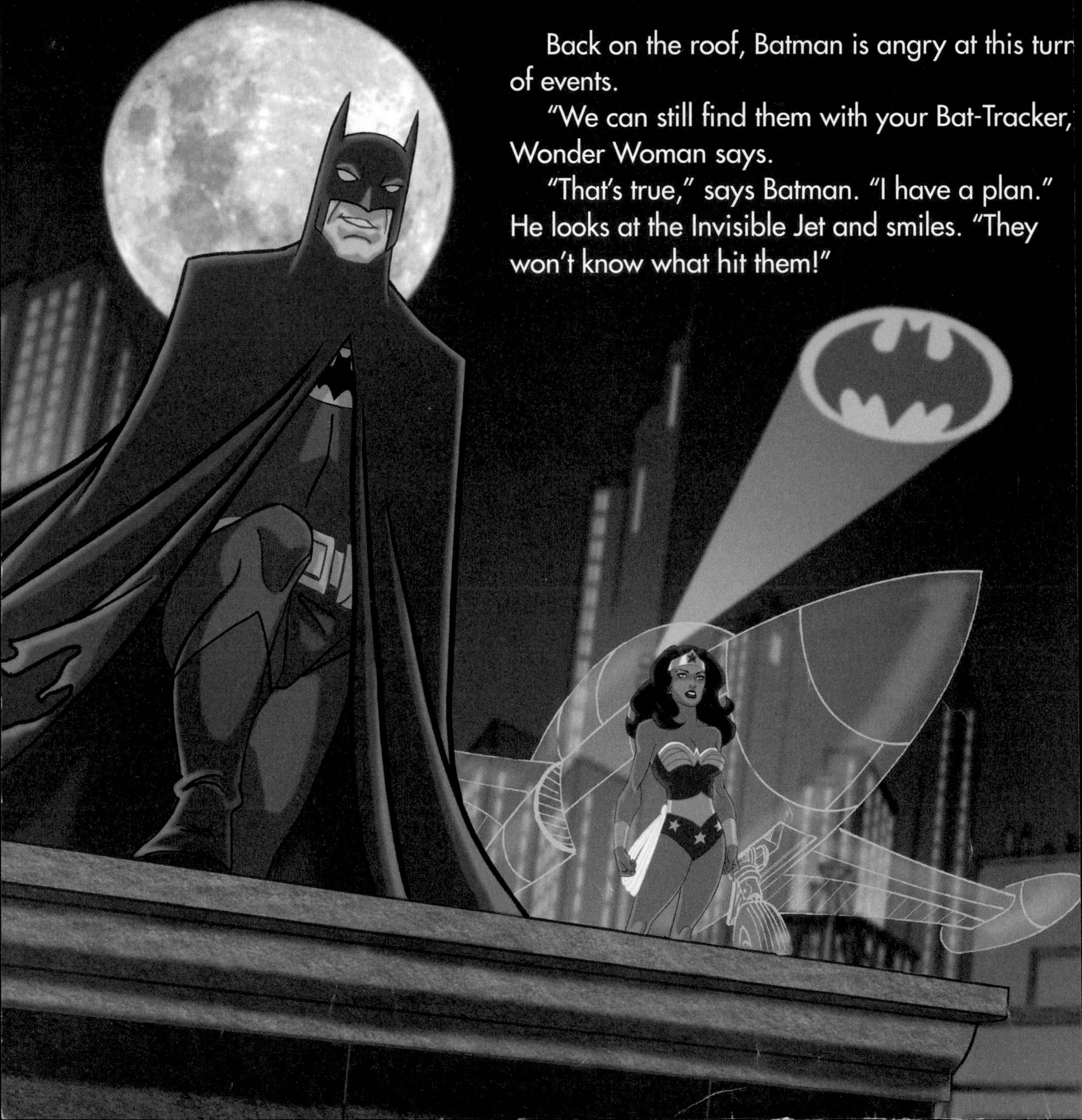

Across town, Catwoman and the Cheetah are now working together to steal the white tiger from the Gotham City Zoo.

"Such a beautiful and powerful creature does not belong in a cage," Catwoman purrs.

"Let's train her to do our bidding!" the Cheetah exclaims.

As Catwoman picks the lock, she is startled by a flying Batarang. The felines scan the darkness but the heroes are nowhere to be seen.

"Show yourself, Batman!" says Catwoman. "I know you found us with some sort of Bat-gadget."

"I bet they're hiding in that blasted Invisible Jet," the Cheetah warns.

"Not anymore," says a voice. Wonder Woman appears behind the Cheetah and knocks her to the ground.

Catwoman cracks her whip at Wonder Woman's feet. The hero twirls her Golden Lasso and says, "Two can play this game!"

The battle is fierce, but Catwoman is no match for the Amazon Princess. She uses her unbreakable lasso to tie up the burglar.

Meanwhile, the Cheetah runs into the lion den. The Caped Crusader emerges from the shadows and swings high overhead. He won't let her get away again.

Batman lands in front of the scoundrel, blocking her escape.
The great cats come to her aid and surround Batman.
"Ready for round two?"
the Cheetah asks, and
prepares to strike.

This time, Batman is faster than the Cheetah. He throws a smoke bomb, releasing a cloud of sleeping gas. When the air clears, *all* the felines are taking a catnap.

Wonder Woman ties the two crooks together while Batman calls the police.
"It's time to put these kittens in a cage," Wonder Woman says.
"There's a big one nearby called Gotham State Prison," Batman replies.
"It's cat-proof!"